The Living Mountain

by Rob Carson

Illustrated by Duane Hoffmann

ISBN 0-9623072-9-7

Published by Storytellers Ink
Seattle, Washington

Printed in the United States of America

CONTENTS

Chapter One
Caravan

"That mountain is never gonna blow up. This is crazy."

A man in a white t-shirt was talking with the policeman at the front of the line. Even from where Laura, Willie and their mother were sitting, several cars back, they could see how annoyed he was.

"We've waited long enough," he was saying. "When are we going to get moving?"

Laura couldn't hear the policeman's answer, but he wasn't smiling. He pointed in the direction of Mount St. Helens poking its snowy top above the trees, and shook his head.

The mountain certainly didn't look as if it could blow up, Laura thought. It looked like a giant mound of vanilla ice cream. She knew just how the man felt.

"Why are they making us wait?" Laura asked. "Catman is up there all alone, probably starving, and we're just sitting here."

"I don't know, honey," Mama said. "But if Catman has lasted this long, another half hour or so is not going to make much difference. They said they would let us go. Now let's just try to be patient."

Laura saw that Mama was worried, too. She was still holding tight to the steering wheel, even though they'd been stopped for a long time and the motor wasn't running.

For two whole weeks, ever since puffs of steam and ash had first started coming out of the mountain, none of the people who owned summer cabins on Spirit Lake had been allowed to go to them.

The scientists who came to study the mountain said the steam coming out the top of the volcano meant it might be ready to erupt, and being as close as Spirit Lake was much too dangerous.

Nobody the Kingsleys knew believed Mount St. Helens would really erupt. Laura's Grandpa Jake, who had built their cabin long before Mama was born, said he'd seen steam plenty of times before and nothing ever happened. Everybody was shocked when the sheriff came up to the cabins and announced that they would have to leave. The sheriff's deputies put a roadblock across the highway to the lake and wouldn't let anybody through except scientists.

The Kingsley's big problem was that their cat, Catman, was up at the cabin all alone. The day the sheriff made them leave, Catman had

gone off somewhere. They had looked and looked, but finally they had to leave without him. No one had been up there to feed him and Laura was worried.

Finally, the sheriff had announced that all the people who owned cabins could go up and get their things. They were all supposed to go up as a group, with the sheriff leading them. Everyone gathered at the roadblock at 10 o'clock in the morning, on time, but now they weren't going anywhere.

"Maybe they're waiting for the helicopter," Willie suggested. "There's supposed to be a helicopter here."

"I don't think that's the reason, honey," Mama said.

Willie was nine, two years younger than Laura. He was okay as little brothers went, but being cooped up in a car with him on a Saturday morning was not Laura's idea of a good time.

Then, sure enough, they heard the faraway "Whop-whop-whop" of a helicopter, and pretty soon they saw it skimming over the trees along the river, racing toward the line of cars.

Willie could hardly contain himself. "See?" he said, "I told you so."

The helicopter hovered over the highway in front of them, making the trees and grass tremble. Willie leaned into the front seat, craning his neck to see out the window.

"Do you mind?" Laura said. She pushed him back.

Up in front of the line, the policeman climbed into his car and switched on his flashing blue lights. He turned his car around so it pointed up the highway. The man who had been pleading with him hurried to his car and got in. Mama turned the key in the ignition. Their old station wagon coughed and gasped but finally started.

"Okay, we're going," she said.

There was a tap on Laura's window. She saw a gloved hand and jumped. It was a policeman. She rolled the window down.

"All set here?" he asked.

Mama nodded. Laura could see her reflection in the policeman's sunglasses.

"Well, okay, we're ready to roll," he said. "Now remember, we'll have exactly three hours up there and that's it. We'll be moving out at two o'clock sharp."

Mama nodded.

The mountain had been Laura's friend for so long, she couldn't imagine it hurting anybody. Every summer she always looked forward to seeing it. The mountain made her feel good inside, and happy. She liked it best when the lake was still and the mountain was reflected in the water, like a mirror. Sometimes she imagined the reflection was part of a whole different upside-down world.

The cars up ahead started moving. Mama released the parking brake. "Put your seatbelts on, please," she told them.

"I have to go to the bathroom," Willie said.

Mama turned and stared at him. "You're kidding."

He shook his head.

Mama sighed and pulled the car out of line. "Well, make it snappy," she said, swinging the car across the road and stopping in front of a little green house with doors that said "Men" and "Women" on them. A dozen or so people were standing around tents nearby. Some of them had binoculars and were looking up at the mountain. Others had cameras.

"You'd better hurry," Laura told Willie. "If we can't get Catman because of you, you're gonna be sorry."

"I can't help it," Willie said. He jumped out of the car and ran.

The people around the tents were laughing and talking. It sounded as if some of them were talking in foreign languages.

"Who are all these people?" Laura asked.

Mama spoke without turning. "Volcano groupies," she said. "I heard somebody talking about them in town. They've come here from all over the world, hoping they'll get to see the mountain blow."

"They *want* it to blow up?" Laura couldn't believe it.

A tall, thin man with black hair and a green backpack hurried up to their car.

"Excuse me ma'am," he said to Mama. "My name is Carlos Crissaros, and I was wondering if I could catch a ride up the mountain with you folks today."

Mama shook her head. "They're only letting people with cabins up there go," she said. "Sorry." She started rolling up her window.

"Oh, wait a second." Carlos slipped his backpack off and rummaged rapidly through one of the pockets. "I should have told you. I'm a scientist. I've got special permission."

He pulled out an official-looking card that read:

"Red Zone Permit/Research."

It had his picture on the front. "I'm supposed to be up there right now, but my car broke down."

"Oh." Mama studied the card. "I thought you're one of these. . . ."

Just then the motor in the station wagon backfired the way it sometimes did. "Ka-blam!"

Laura flinched. Some of the people around the tents crouched down, holding their heads. Others stared up at the mountain, mouths open, thinking it had exploded.

Willie running, yanking on his pants, said: "What's going on?"

"Oh, nothing," Laura told him. "Our car just erupted, that's all."

The last car in the caravan had just pulled away, and the last police car was waiting for them. "Come on, ma'am," the policeman shouted. "Let's move it."

Willie jumped in the back seat, and Carlos stood there alone, his permit card in his hands.

"Okay, hop in," Mama told him. "But we won't be able to bring you back down. We're going to have the car full of our stuff."

"That's great," Carlos said, climbing in, and folding his long legs up like a grasshopper. "I'll catch a ride down with somebody else."

As they swung into line, the last police car pulled in behind them, its lights flashing. Overhead, the helicopter buzzed back and forth.

Laura gazed out the window at the mountain until it disappeared behind a hillside covered with tall fir trees. "We're coming, Catman," she said to herself.

Chapter Two
Carlos

The caravan of cars wound slowly up the narrow road that followed the Toutle River to the volcano. Since nobody else could get past the roadblocks, they had the whole road to themselves. On big curves, Laura could see all the rest of the cars lined up ahead of them, moving together like cars on a train. The police car in front, with its blue lights flashing, was like the engine. The police car behind them was like the caboose.

Laura had expected things to look different than usual but she couldn't see that anything had changed at all. The river flashed over rocks, clear and clean as always. Pink and red rhododendrons peeked through the trees at the edge of the forest, and once she caught a glimpse of a deer and two fawns standing like statues in the trees, watching them drive by.

Could the animals that lived up here — the deer, raccoons, squirrels, birds, and all the other creatures — know that they lived next to a volcano, Laura wondered?

Carlos, as it turned out, was not a full-fledged scientist yet, but a student from Cuernavaca, Mexico, in his last year of graduate school at the University of Washington. He was helping his professor do a study that involved, as far as Laura could tell, marking off big squares on the ground and counting everything that lived in them — every plant and every animal, right down to the smallest bug — both above the ground and below it, too.

"It's amazing," Carlos was saying. "Although we've been living next to these amazing forests for generations, nobody has ever taken the time to document exactly what lives in them. We're trying to find everything that's here now so that we can see how it all changes after the eruption."

"After the eruption?" Mama said. "That's quite an assumption, isn't it? For a scientist?"

"Not really," Carlos said. "Everybody knows the mountain is going to erupt again sooner or later. The only question is when. Historically, it's erupted around every hundred and fifty years, and it's been about that long since the last time. There's no reason to think the pattern will change because people happen to live around here now."

"How do you know it's erupted before?" Willie demanded, leaning up from the back seat.

"You can tell from from the rocks and other stuff," Carlos said. "Like, look right there." He pointed to a wall of hard-packed dirt at the side of the road. "See all those stripes? The brown ones, the black ones and the sort of gray ones?" Mama slowed down and they all looked. There were stripes. Laura was surprised she'd never noticed them before. They looked like layers in a huge piece of cake.

"Those layers show every volcanic eruption." Carlos said. "The gray ones are from when the ash came flying out. The brown ones are from mud that flowed down when the ice and snow melted. And the black ones are soil from the stuff that grew in between eruptions.

"But, couldn't it be just a little eruption?" Mama asked. "Couldn't it just shoot up little bursts of steam and then quit?"

"It could. And a lot of people think that's just what's going to happen. But, it could just as easily be a big one."

"One thing is for sure," Carlos said. "They've got this mountain so wired up with equipment, they know every time it gives the slightest little burp or wiggle."

"So they'll know if it's going to erupt?"

"Usually right before an eruption, there'll be a lot of little quakes coming from the mountain. They come faster and faster and then, a few days or so before it erupts, they come really fast. That's when you know it's about to blow and you had better get out of the way."

"Sometimes volcanoes will just settle down again. They're hard to predict. Anyway, I should tell you, my specialty is living things — you know, plants and animals — not rocks. If you really want to know all the details you should talk to a geologist."

Plants and animals, Laura thought with a flash. He would know about cats. Shyly, she tapped Carlos' shoulder. "How long can a cat live without food?" She asked.

Carlos didn't seem to have any difficulty going from volcanoes to cats. "Wild or domesticated?" he asked her.

Laura wasn't sure what "domesticated" meant. "Well, like a kitty cat," she said.

"I would think, oh, I'd say at least two weeks, providing they had water of course, and . . ." Laura saw Mama give Carlos a warning look out of the corner of her eye. ". . . And, ah . . . the thing to remember about cats is that they're good hunters, and there's lots of fresh water around. Cats could catch a lot of food and do just fine."

Mama nodded. "That's what I've been telling her."

Laura realized they were just trying to keep her from worrying. If Catman could catch mice or something, maybe he'd be all right.

If not . . . she couldn't think about it. Catman was pretty tough, though. When they first met him he didn't cautiously sneak up to their house like a regular cat would have. No. He just stomped right up as if he owned the place, and said something like "Roairoww."

They had all laughed and Mama said "He's a fierce little guy, isn't he?" So they started calling him Catman and it stuck. He kept coming around more and more, and after a while he just stayed.

"What makes volcanoes, anyway?" Willie asked.

Laura stared at Willie. He said he was worried about Catman, but he sure didn't act like it. He couldn't stop talking about volcanoes.

"Well," Carlos said, "I'm a plants–and–animals guy, but the way I understand it, it's like this. Way, way down under the ground, in the core of the earth, it is very hot. It's so hot, the rock there is melted."

"You mean like in a blast furnace, where they melt steel."

"Yes, like that, only the melted stuff is everywhere, like a super hot ocean. And the ground is just floating around on that ocean of melted rock, like, oh, like what?" Carlos thought for a moment. "Like if you poured a bunch of marshmallows in a bathtub full of water."

"But what makes volcanoes explode?"

"Well, remember, it's not marshmallows we're talking about, but huge amounts of rock — miles and miles thick — like forty miles. So, when these big chunks of rock grind into each other, they create this incredible force. That pressure has to go somewhere, so it rises up through the cracks in the earth to the top, and 'Boom!' Out it comes."

Willie looked puzzled. "But why does it always happen at the top of a mountain?"

"The volcano actually makes the mountain, not the other way around," Carlos explained. "What the mountain really is, is all that rock and stuff that shoots out during an eruption. It cools down and hardens. After years and years and years of it erupting and cooling, there's a huge pile of it, and that's what we call mountains."

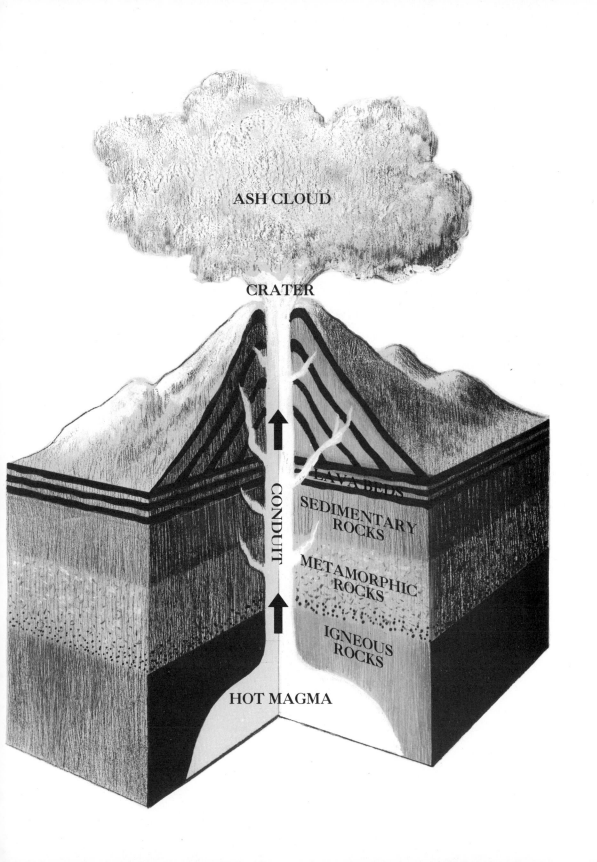

ASH CLOUD

CRATER

CONDUIT

LAVA BEDS

SEDIMENTARY
ROCKS

METAMORPHIC
ROCKS

IGNEOUS
ROCKS

HOT MAGMA

They had reached the last big wooden bridge over the Toutle
River, the one that had always meant to Laura and Willie that they
were almost at the lake. Just after the bridge they would get their first
really good view of the mountain, reflected in the water. It was a
magical moment and one they always looked forward to.

Laura usually tried to hold her breath from the time they crossed
the bridge until she saw the mountain, but today, she couldn't do it.
The caravan was moving too slowly. She gave a big gasp after she let
her air out and Carlos looked at her — puzzled. She just smiled at him.

Mama spotted the mountain first. "There it is," she said, pointing
out the front window. Mount St. Helens rose above them, so big it
almost looked like a wall. Laura noticed that the snow on top, usually
pure white, was dark and stained.

"Hey," Willie said. "It's all dirty."

"Ash," Carlos said. "That's the stuff that's been shooting out the
top. Look around, it's all over everything up here."

Laura looked, and sure enough, the leaves on all the trees looked dusty. On the road, the car tires were making tracks on the pavement.

Carlos started thanking them for the ride as soon as they saw the first cabin, and he kept telling them how much he appreciated it all the way to the Spirit Lake parking lot. There, he got out and headed uphill to where he was supposed to meet the other scientists.

"Thanks again," he said.

"Thank you for the geology lesson," Mama said. Mama was glad they had given him a ride, Laura could tell by her smile.

The policeman who had been driving the first car got out and gathered everyone together. "Okay, now remember," he told them. "Two o'clock sharp. That's when we're pulling out. Do not be late."

"Should be plenty of time," Mama said. She drove down the main road and turned onto the dirt driveway that led to the cabin.

"As long as we can find Catman," Laura thought.

19

Chapter Three
Catman

Laura had never heard it so quiet around the cabin before. It was eerie. There were no boats gliding through the water and no birds chirping in the trees.

Crunching down the gravel path to the cabin, the only sound Laura could hear was the humming of honeybees in the flowers — and Willie, of course.

"Pleeease, Mom," he was pleading. "It took me years to find all those rocks. We can't just leave them here."

"If we have enough room, we can take some of them," Mama said. "I know it took a lot of time to find them all, but I just don't think everything is going to fit. We have to decide what is most important.

The path and all the trees and bushes were covered with a light coat of dusty ash. Laura brushed her hand across the top of a leaf and studied the gray powder on her fingertips. It looked like dirty flour.

Laura took the path that went around the side of the cabin, to the hole in the wall where Catman could go in and out when he wanted to. "Catman," she called. "Catman. . . we're back!"

She made a big loop around the cabin, then scooted down the path that dropped to the beach, calling Catman's name.

When she got back to the cabin, she stuck her head under the front porch, where it was cool and dark. "Come on, Catman," she said. "We're sorry."

Willie and Mama came out of the cabin to help look, but after calling once or twice, Willie gave up and went down to the beach. Laura saw that he was throwing rocks, trying to hit the float they dove off when it was warm enough to swim. Mama walked back and forth, clapping her hands like she did when she called Catman for dinner.

Laura was just getting ready to go inside and get some cat food so she could rattle it around in Catman's dish, when she heard an indignant, "Reeroww," near the rowboat.

There was Catman, striding toward her. He looked as good as ever, maybe even a little better. He wasn't a bit skinny and his fur was nice and thick and glossy.

"Catman!" Laura cried. She ran and picked him up. Then she sat down on the grass and held him on her lap, rocking back and forth. He purred and pawed her chest with his front feet. It was a habit that usually bothered Laura, but now she was happy to let him do it. "They wouldn't let us wait for you," she explained. "We didn't forget you; they wouldn't let us come back."

"Mama," she called. "I found him!"

"How is he?" Mama asked, hurrying toward her.

"He looks wonderful," Laura said. She put her head down close to Catman's and talked softly. "You must be a terrific hunter, aren't you, Catman. Such a talented kitty."

Mama looked him over. "Amazing," she said. "What do you suppose he's been eating? He looks healthier than ever."

Willie came up from the beach, staggering under the weight of a huge rock. "Oh, good, you found him," he said. "Hiya, Catman."

Mama turned back toward the cabin. "Well," she said. "I better start getting things packed up. Laura, I think you and Willie could help most by just staying outside until I get everything in boxes. Then we'll all help carry them to the car."

Laura nodded. That was fine with her.

"And by all means, keep an eye on Catman," Mama said. "Don't let him run off somewhere again. We've all got to be ready to go, and in the car, in . . ." she looked at her watch . . ."two hours and thirty minutes."

Willie immediately headed back down to the beach. Laura sat on the grass with Catman and gazed at the reflection of Mount St. Helens in the lake. The ripples in the water seemed to shatter the mountain into thousands of shimmering pieces. Laura tried to imagine it blowing up. Would the top just open up, and hot stuff come shooting out? It seemed impossible.

Laura decided to take one last ride on the swing on the big fir tree.

A great old swing that had been there long before Laura was born. Mama told her she used to swing on it herself when she was a little girl. They'd had to replace the ropes a couple of times, but that was all.

Laura carried Catman over and put him down by the tree. The swing seat was covered with ash, so she turned it over and wiped the dust off before she sat down. As she got higher, she watched the mountain, rising up over the tops of the trees when she went forward, and then dropping back down when she went back.

After a few minutes she looked down at where Catman had been. He was gone.

"Darn it," she said.

Laura dragged her feet in the dirt under the swing and jumped off.

"Catman," she said, looking quickly around. "Catman!"

She glanced up at the cabin just in time to see the cat go around the corner and head up the gravel path, glancing over his shoulder as he went.

Chapter Four
Harry

Laura rushed up the path and into the trees, not wanting to lose sight of Catman. Her eyes weren't used to the dark forest and she couldn't see anything at first — especially not a little cat. She blinked and then squinted for a second or two until her eyes adjusted. Then she saw Catman veer off the main trail and dart to the right.

"Catman!" she called after him, "You come back here right now."

Catman stopped, but he didn't come back. He sat down and looked at Laura as she hurried toward him.

"Reeoww," he said.

Laura got so close she could almost touch him. "That's a good kitty," she said. Slowly, she knelt down to pick him up. At that very moment, Catman leaped away from her and ran deeper into the woods, following an overgrown trail that Laura had seen but had never taken.

"Catman," Laura said, following along behind him. "Where do you think you're going? You don't want to stay up here all by yourself again, do you? We're leaving today, you know." She tried to sound stern, but it wasn't easy because she was out of breath from running.

Catman went on ahead, stopping occasionally to meow. Just when she would get close to him, he would leap away and run ahead. Then he would stop and wait for her until she caught up again.

Soon Laura was a long way from the cabin. She stopped and thought. Should she keep on going and try to catch Catman herself? Or should she go back and get Mama and Willie to help? If she left him up here in the woods, they would never be able to find him again. And Mama had told her to watch him. She decided to keep on going at least a little farther.

The trail climbed away from the lake shore and into bigger trees, a place that Laura was pretty sure was what everybody called Cathedral Forest. It looked like it, anyway. The trees were giants here, as big around as cars. The air was cool under them, even though it was a sunny day. Big lacy ferns with drooping leaves covered the ground and made perfect hiding places for cats. It was very quiet. Laura couldn't see Catman anywhere. She kept walking, calling his name as she went.

The old trail branched off into two trails, and then branched again. The first time Laura stayed on the bigger one, but the second time the two trails were about the same size and she couldn't decide which one to take. She stopped and studied them. One was flatter and looked as if it would be easier to walk on, but the other one, overgrown and winding, looked more like someplace a cat would want to go. She chose that one. And she was glad she did because pretty soon she heard rustling in the ferns and out popped Catman, so close she almost stepped on him.

"There you are, you naughty cat," Laura said. She knelt to pick him up and he was gone again, bounding out of the trees and into a clearing ahead, where the bright sun was shining on green grass.

Laura followed him into the sunlight and suddenly stopped. There in front of her was a large building. It was painted green with red window trim and had tall peaked roofs. Somehow, she had ended up at Spirit Lake Lodge, old Harry Truman's place.

The only times she had been there before was when they ran out of milk or something else they had to have. Then Mama always drove.

Harry lived in the lodge by himself and rented out boats and sold food, gas and fishing supplies in the summer. Sometimes she'd see him driving around in his car—an old pink Cadillac with gold wire wheels. Some kids were afraid of Harry, but Mama said he was nice. When the sheriff ordered everybody to leave the lake, Harry had refused.

Laura heard meows coming from the front of the lodge, but they didn't sound like Catman. Quietly, tiptoeing in the grass, she walked around the corner of the lodge.

In front of the lodge, cracked red concrete steps led up to an old wooden porch. There were cats everywhere—yellow cats, brown cats, grey cats and black cats—arching their backs, scratching the porch floor, meowing and twitching their tails. And right there among them was Catman.

Laura started foward, hoping she could grab him before Harry saw her. She got as far as the bottom step when Harry came out the front door. He was wearing a baseball cap, and his hair, what she could see of it under the cap, was pure white. He was walking backward, dragging an enormous bag of cat food.

Harry didn't see her. "Come and get it, you fleabags," he said to the cats. The cats surrounded him. Catman rubbed up against his leg.

Harry reached inside the bag and took out a handful of cat food. He tossed it out on the steps, spreading it among the cats so they could all get some. "That's right," he said. "Eat up, boys and girls. It's chowtime." He tossed out handful after handful, until the red steps were brown with cat food.

No wonder Catman looked so healthy, Laura thought. He'd been eating at Harry's place this whole time. Some hunter.

Harry still hadn't seen her. Laura thought she should let him know she was there so she made a little coughing noise to get his attention.

Harry squinted over in her direction, startled. "Who's that?"

Laura came a little closer. "Laura Kingsley," she said.

Harry stared at her. "Jake Kingsley's kid?"

"Grandpa. I mean, his grandkid," Laura stammered. "He's my grandpa."

Harry reached back into the sack for another handful of cat food. "What are you doing up here?" he said. "Aren't you afraid the mountain is gonna blow, like everybody else?"

"We came to get our cat." Laura said. She pointed at Catman, busily crunching cat chow. "That one."

Harry squatted down and rubbed the top of Catman's head with a crooked finger. "This guy?" Harry picked him up. "I wondered where he came from."

Harry didn't say anything for a while. He watched the cats eat. "I don't know how people can go off and leave their pets all by themselves," he said shaking his head.

"We didn't mean to," Laura said quickly. "He ran off and then they made us leave. They closed the road and wouldn't let us come back up here."

She hoped he wasn't mad. "Thank you very much for taking care of him," she added politely.

Harry stood up. "They tried to kick me out, too," he said, "but I told 'em I wasn't going. The sheriff stood right where you're standing. I told him he'd better get out the handcuffs 'cause I'm staying put."

Laura nodded. "They only just let us up here today to get our stuff. Now we have to go right back down again." Laura remembered what the policeman had said about being on time. She wondered what time it was. "I better get back right now," she said.

Laura looked down at Catman and all the rest of the cats. They reminded her of a flock of pigeons in the park, eating bread crumbs.

"You must really like cats," she said.

Harry shrugged. "Somebody's got to feed 'em. Anyway, only sixteen of 'em are mine. The rest just kind of found me. Like yours." Harry looked at her closely. "Jake's kid, huh?"

"Granddaughter," Laura said.

Harry wiped his hands on his pants. "Well," he said, "I guess the least I can do for Jake is to offer his kid something to drink. You want a bottle of pop or something?"

Laura was suddenly very thirsty. In fact, now that she thought about it, she could hardly swallow, she was so thirsty. It was hot, and she had walked a long way.

"Well, I guess I could use a drink before we go," she said.

"Okay, c'mon in."

He dragged the bag of cat food back into the lodge and Laura followed him cautiously, with Catman following, her shoes crunching on cat food.

Inside, Laura found herself in a big room with an old leather couch and a couple of chairs around a stone fireplace. One wall was covered with old photographs in frames. Out the window she could see the lake and Mount St. Helens, so big she couldn't see the top of it.

Harry reappeared with a bottle of orange soda and a coke.
He handed her the bottle of orange and kept the coke for himself.

Catman strode past them and went into a room Laura thought
must be the kitchen.

Another cat, sitting in a cardboard box in the doorway hissed
half-heartedly at Catman and then slinked away.

Laura sipped the orange soda. It was warm, but sweet and fizzy.
She looked out the window and saw the old pink Cadillac sitting by
itself under a tree. It was covered with gray dust, like everything else.
Suddenly, things seemed scary, with the mountain so big and dark, the
car gray.

"What if they're right?" she blurted out.

Harry looked surprised. "What if who's right?" he said.

"The scientists and everybody else. What if the mountain does
blow up?"

"Well, then I guess it will blow up, that's all."

"It really could, you know."

"I suppose."

"And if it does, you'll be . . . you'll be here, and you'll be . . ."

Laura had trouble saying what she meant. "You could really be hurt. Aren't you scared?"

"Scared?" Harry said the word as if he was trying to remember what it meant. "Honey, when you've lived as long as I have there's not much left that can scare you."

He went over to the wall of pictures. Squinting at them, he found the one he wanted and put his finger on it. "Come look at this."

It was a picture of a man and a little boy standing on a dock at the lake. Laura didn't recognize any of them, but the man looked a little like Harry.

"That one's me," he said. "Guess who the kid is."

Laura shook her head. She had no idea.

"That's your grandpa." Harry said.

Laura studied the picture. "But he's old now, and you're . . . "

". . . a whole lot older." Harry nodded his head. "When you've lived as long as I have, you look at things differently. You realize it's not the end of the world if things change. And that includes mountains blowing up."

Harry sat down at the table and took a sip of his coke. "That mountain's been up there, blowing her stack and then settling down again for so long, it's no big deal to her. It's like the seasons changing. It's what's supposed to happen. The end of one thing is just the beginning of something else, that's all."

Laura felt dizzy all of a sudden. The room felt as if it were moving. Their glasses slid across the table and the pictures rattled on the wall. One of them fell off its hook and smashed on the floor. Laura grabbed the back of the couch to keep from falling over. "What's happening?" she cried.

Harry put his hands on the glasses to keep them from sliding off. Laura held on tight to the couch. The jars and boxes on Harry's shelves rattled and shook. A box of sugar fell off the counter and spilled on the floor. Laura heard herself scream. Catman raced across the room and out the door. Then the movement stopped.

Laura looked out the window at the mountain, expecting to see smoke coming out the top or hot lava running down its sides. It looked the same, as far as she could tell. She could hardly speak. "Is it blowing up?" she managed to ask.

"Nah," Harry said. "That was just an earthquake."

It's been doing this for two months. There's been hundreds of them. It got so bad I had to move my bed down to the basement so I could get some sleep."

"I've got to go now," Laura said. Suddenly, getting into the car with Mama and Willie and heading back home seemed like the most important thing in the world. She hurried to the door. Catman was sitting alone on the steps. All the other cats were gone. She went to him and he let her pick him up without any problem.

"Can you find your way back?" Harry said from the doorway. Laura nodded.

"Those trails get pretty snarled up back there."

"No, I'll be okay."

"Okay, then," he said. He touched the brim of his cap. And then, so softly Laura could hardly hear him, he added, "Good luck, little lady."

Chapter Five
Finding the Trail

Carrying Catman turned out to be almost impossible. He was a big cat, and heavy. But that wasn't the worst part. He wanted to walk. And he kept squirming in Laura's arms.

"I've got to carry you, Catman, or you'll just run away," Laura told him, hugging him tighter to her chest. "It's your own fault. You did it before, you know."

"Reeooow," Catman pleaded, looking into her eyes.

Laura kept on walking. "I can't, Catman," she said. "You might just run away again, and then what would we do? We'd have to leave you behind again."

"Reeah-reooow," Catman argued.

Talking and meowing to each other, Laura and Catman made it to the place where the trail split in two. Laura took the one that went to the right, because she was sure that she had been on the trail that was more beaten down with footprints.

The next time the trail divided, she wasn't quite so sure. She stood at the place where one path, a rather leafy one, headed uphill, and a rutted, muddy one headed down.

She tried to remember how she had come, but it looked different going backwards. She was deep in the woods by this time and couldn't see the mountain or the lake. Nor could she decide which way to go.

"Which way here, Catman?" she asked. "You've done this a hundred times I bet, haven't you?"

Catman didn't say anything, so Laura gently set him on the ground, right where the trail divided. She kept her hands around his middle so he couldn't escape. Instantly, he started for the leafy trail.

"Thank you, Catman." Laura picked him up again and turned onto the leafy trail. "I was hoping that was the one you'd pick."

"It can't be much farther," Laura told him. "Hang on a little longer and we'll be home safe and sound with Mama again.

But it wasn't just a little farther, and nothing looked familiar. They seemed to be going uphill more than Laura remembered. She decided they must be on the wrong trail. "I don't want to blame you, Catman," she said, "but do you think it's possible you might have

goofed back there?" Laura turned around and they headed back to the place where the trail divided.

She walked and walked, for longer than she thought it should have taken them to get back. But she couldn't find the fork in the trail. Instead, she found a different fork. Now Laura was getting worried. Mama must have finished packing by now and she was probably out looking for her. She would be mad. What would the policeman say?

"Okay, Catman. I'm going to give you another chance. Which way here?" She held him on the trail again. This time, though, Catman gave a sudden twist — jumped out of her hands — and hit the ground running. "Rioww," he said and disappeared into the underbrush.

"Hey! Wait a minute!" Laura stumbled after him, but Catman was gone. "Catman," she called. "Catman. Wait for me."

There was no answer. Laura stopped and listened carefully to see if she could hear leaves rustling as he ran. Everything was quiet.

Laura was all alone and didn't have any idea where she was. Up until then she had a feeling she knew where the lake was at least, and where the volcano was, but now, she couldn't be sure. All she could see were trees.

"I'm lost. I really am lost." She said the words out loud, not quite believing them. Laura had been lost before, but always in town, where she could ask people or read signs or, once when she had been really confused, call her mother from a pay phone. But here . . . there was nobody to help her.

Laura felt shaky. "Let's just keep calm," she told herself. But it didn't help. Inside she was scared. The lake must be downhill, she thought. She would just keep going downhill, and sooner or later she was sure to end up at the lake. Then she could see where she was.

Laura was so sure that this was the right thing to do that she hurried faster and faster downhill. Soon she found herself running through the trees. Branches and bushes whipped against her as she ran, stinging her arms and face.

She was breathing so hard her lungs hurt. She wanted to stop running, but she couldn't. I'm panicking, she thought. But she just couldn't make herself slow down.

Suddenly, the forest floor dropped out from under her. Just ahead was a rock cliff, too steep to go down. Just in time, she sat down on the ground above it.

She could hear water running down below. Her arms were scratched and her hair wet in her face. Now what?

Somewhere, far away, she heard horns honking. Little tiny horns and big deep angry horns, all honking at once. They must be honking at her, Laura realized. Everybody in the caravan is all ready to go and they're wondering where I am.

It was impossible to tell exactly where the sounds were coming from. It sounded as if they might be behind her, or up in the sky.

Just then she heard the helicopter again, somewhere above her. It was flying in circles. Maybe they're looking for me, Laura thought. But then the sound grew fainter and fainter. Laura's heart sank. The helicopter was leading the caravan away from the lake, she realized. They're leaving me, Laura thought.

Laura thought about the Indian boys Grandpa had told her about, the ones that lived here long ago. When they were about her age, Grandpa said, their parents sent them all alone high up the mountain where they believed the Great Spirit lived. They would spend the whole night there by themselves. If they were brave enough not to come running down, the parents figured they were ready to be adults.

Laura wondered if the Indian kids felt the way she was feeling. She bet they thought about sasquatches, the big creatures that everybody used to think lived up here, the ones who were half ape and half man. All the grown-ups thought it was fun to talk about them in soft, scary voices late at night around campfires. Mama had never done that. She always said that it was all a bunch of nonsense. Laura didn't believe in sasquatches.

Even so, it was hard to keep from thinking about them. She decided waiting to be found wasn't the right idea. It made more sense to keep going downhill to the bottom of the cliff. If the water she heard was a creek, she'd follow it because it should flow into the lake.

Laura faced the cliff and started down backward, searching for places to put her feet and hands. "This isn't so bad," she was thinking, when all of a sudden one end of a root she was holding broke loose, and she slid down the hill. She rolled and slid over rocks and tree stumps. She reached out and tried to grab things as she went, but she was moving too fast. With a bump, she landed at the bottom, sprawled out on her stomach. She wiggled her toes and moved her fingers and neck to see if she was all right. Everything still seemed to be working.

She lay there, not moving for a long time. Then, not far away, she heard a noise in the bushes. A rustling noise, like something alive. It was coming toward her. A deer? No, it was too noisy. A cougar? No, they were even quieter. A bear? Maybe, but it was taking long heavy steps . . . it was more like a sasquatch! One of them was going to get her and eat her.

The footsteps got closer and closer. Step, step, step . . . Laura tried to scream, but she couldn't make any sound come out. The bushes moved right next to her, and out stepped Carlos.

He was as surprised to see her as she was to see him. "Laura!" he said. "What the . . .?"

Laura couldn't talk. She just looked at him, trying to keep from crying. Carlos knelt down beside her. He smoothed the hair out of her face. "You're all scratched up," he said. "Are you okay?"

Laura nodded.

"I heard on the radio that a little girl was missing, but I never thought it would be you," he said. "How did you get way over here?"

Laura managed to tell him all about Catman running away, and Harry, and how she was trying to go downhill where she thought the lake would be.

"Well, you had the right idea," Carlos said. "This stream does go to the lake. But you're way past the cabins. You must have gone up too far and passed right by them."

Carlos had been on his way down from the volcano to help look for her. He unhooked the radio from his belt and put it up to his mouth, holding down a button.

"Spirit Lake, this is Carlos," he said into it.

There was some static and a click and then a man's scratchy voice. "Yeah, Carlos."

"I found her. I've got her right here and she's okay."

There was a pause. Then, "Great, okay. Ten-four. That's good.

Ah, what's your ten-twenty, Carlos?"

"We're about, oh, a quarter of a mile up Silver Creek," he said into the radio. "We should be down there in fifteen minutes."

"That's great, Carlos. I'll call everybody off. You need any help?"

"No, we're fine. We'll just walk in," Carlos said.

"Can you ask them about Catman?" Laura said.

Carlos hesitated and then nodded. He pushed the button again. "Ah, Spirit Lake?"

"Yeah, Carlos?"

"Ah, do you have a ten-twenty on the cat?"

"That's affirmative," the scratchy voice said. "He's right here with the mother. We're all here waiting for you."

"Ten-four," Carlos said, giving Laura a big smile. "Over and out."

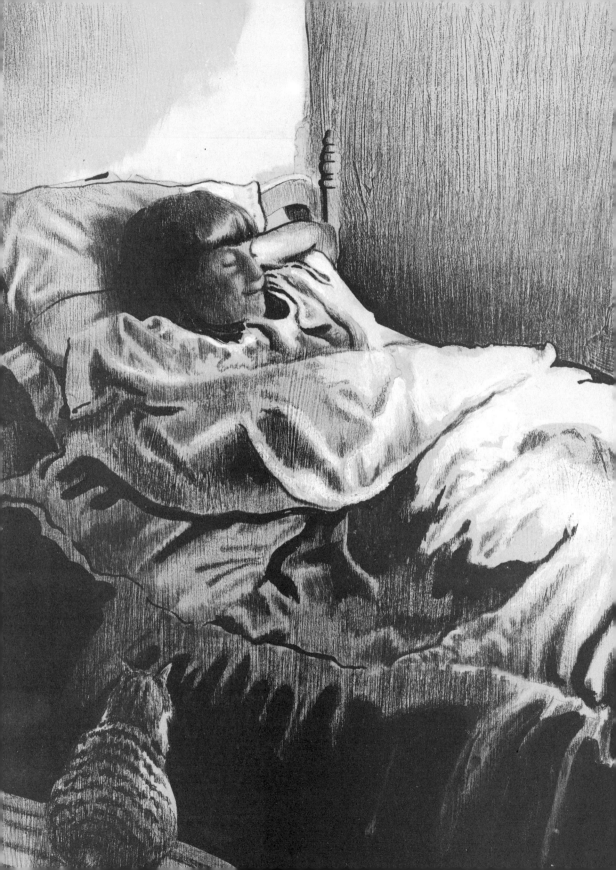

Chapter Six
Eruption

Laura yawned and stretched her arms up over her head. It was time
to get up, but it felt so good in bed that she didn't want to. How wonderful sheets and blankets and pillows were, she thought. Somebody
had a very good idea when they invented them. She tried imagining for
a minute what it would have been like if Carlos hadn't come along
yesterday and she had to spend the night out on the hard, cold ground.
She shivered and wrapped the blankets tighter around her.

Catman was glad to be home, too. Last night he hadn't wanted to
sleep in his box. He wanted to be in Laura's room, close to her. He
was still there now, sitting on the hooked rug, washing himself with
his tongue.

Laura loved Sunday mornings. Mama didn't have to work, and
even if she had a big test or something coming up, she always spent the
whole morning with Laura and Willie. They had a special breakfast,

with either French toast or pancakes, and nobody was allowed to watch any television. That had been the rule ever since Daddy left and Mama started working at the restaurant.

Laura examined the scratches on her arms. Not too bad really, she thought. They'd be gone in no time.

Willie was up already. Laura could hear him in the kitchen, pestering Mama to make banana pancakes for breakfast instead of French toast.

At breakfast, they talked about old Harry Truman. Willie said, "It seems kind of dumb for him to stay up there, with the mountain about to blow up."

"Somebody said he told them he had a secret place up there, a cave or an old mine where he was going to go if it starts erupting," Mama said.

"Really?" Laura was interested. Harry hadn't mentioned anything about it to her.

"They said he called it his 'hidey hole.' He's supposed to have food and water stashed up there. They said if something starts he'll just go in there with all his cats and wait until it's over."

"That's what I'd do," Willie said.

Somebody knocked on the front door. Willie dropped his fork and ran to open it, wiping his sticky hands on the front of his shirt.

He swung the door open. "Mama, it's that scientist guy."

"Carlos?" Laura said. "What's he doing here?"

Mama got up quickly and walked to the door.

Carlos was excited. "Wow," he said. "Talk about great timing."

"Timing?" Mama looked puzzled.

"I mean, getting all your stuff out yesterday, just in time."

"In time for what?"

"You didn't hear?"

"Hear what?" Laura asked.

"The mountain blew up!" Carlos took a step back onto the porch and held the screen door open for them. "Take a look."

They all went out on the porch with Carlos. Willie pushed his way out first. Carlos pointed to the sky, over the roofs of the houses across the street. They couldn't see the mountain itself from where they were. But up in the sky Laura saw a huge billowing cloud. It was the only cloud in the sky and it was moving — tumbling around as if it were alive. It looked weird, like a speeded-up movie of storm clouds. Except this was really happening. Laura felt dizzy watching it, like she had yesterday at Harry's place. She grabbed onto the porch railing to keep steady. It was beautiful and terrible at the same time.

"Oh, my gosh," Mama said.

They all stared up at it. "It went off at 8:21 this morning," Carlos said quietly. "A huge eruption. Bigger than anybody thought it would be. The whole north side of the mountain is gone, they think."

"I didn't hear a thing," Mama said. "I was up at seven. There weren't any booms or anything."

"It's something weird about the way sound travels," Carlos said. "I didn't hear it either. But lots of other people did. They said it sounded like a bunch of cannons going off, or thunder."

"Is it going to get us?" Willie asked. His voice sounded strange. Laura looked at her brother for the first time since they had gone outside. She realized that was the first thing he'd said since he'd barged out ahead of them. He was standing close to Mama and hanging onto her sweatshirt with one hand. He was scared.

"No," Carlos said. He got down and talked right at Willie, but Laura could tell he was talking to her and Mama, too. "It's not going to get us," he said. "We're 50 miles away. Everything is going in the other direction." He looked up at Mama. "You can be glad you're not up at the cabin right now though, that's for sure."

An awful thought struck Laura. "What about Harry?" she said.

Carlos looked at her for a second and then looked down at the porch. He shook his head. "Nobody knows anything for sure yet. It's hard to say. It doesn't look good though."

Laura got a clear picture in her mind of Harry's face, all whiskery, talking to her from across his kitchen table. No way could he be gone, she thought. He's too real.

"Everything is very confused up there," Carlos said. "Nobody knows what's going on. None of the pilots can see anything. No one can even get close."

Carlos was driving a Forest Service truck and was on his way to the place where all the rescue teams were meeting. Laura and Willie and Mama walked with him to the street.

"You're sure we're okay here, right?" Mama asked.

"As long as the wind keeps blowing that way, you're fine. If it switches, we'll get some ash falling. The main thing to look out for on this side is the mudflows."

"Mudflows?" Mama said.

"All that heat up there is going to melt the snow and ice. When it mixes with the ash, everything can come shooting down the mountain. You should keep an eye on the river."

After Carlos drove off, Laura, Willie and Mama went back inside the house and closed the door. They sat in the living room and looked out the big window at the cloud, and all the people out watching it.

"Now what?" Laura said.

"Wait, I guess," Mama said. "I don't know. Watch the river?"

Laura couldn't see what the river could possibly do to them. It was not that big and it was four blocks away, all the way down by the school. What harm could mud do anyway?

"Can we go out and watch it?" Willie said. He didn't seem to be scared anymore.

Mama shook her head.

"After yesterday, I'm not letting you out of my sight."

It seemed strange to stay in the house with a volcano blowing up outside. "Then you come with us, Mama," Laura said. "Carlos said to keep an eye on the river. From the school we could see the mountain and the river, too."

Mama got up. "Okay," she said. "Let's see what's going on."

They weren't the only ones who had the idea about going to the school. The playground was crowded with people. Most were looking down the bank at the river.

As they got closer they could hear a roar that sounded like heavy traffic. They walked over to the edge where everyone was.

Laura looked at the river and gasped. It was ten times higher than it normally was. It looked like wet cement not water. Bunches of huge trees were racing by, bouncing and crashing into each other in the mud. What looked like half a house was on its way around the bend.

Suddenly they noticed three horses in the muddy water, just off the bank swimming together, their heads barely above the water.

A man was trying to get a rope around the closest ones' neck, and another man managed to grab the mane of one and pulled himself onto its' back. Somehow he turned the horse back toward shore and the other two horses followed until they had their footing.

They couldn't see the volcano anymore. The sky was gray. Laura took her mother's hand in hers. Mama smiled at her. "Let's go back home," she said.

"I hope Harry made it to his hidey hole," Laura said.

"I wouldn't count on it," a voice behind them said. Laura turned around. It was a skinny man with a camera around his neck. "I was just talking to some guys who were listening to the radio and they said Spirit Lake is gone totally. The whole lake. Poof. Just blown away. That old guy doesn't stand a chance."

Chapter Seven
Summer

Laura and Willie's school was closed for two weeks. Lots of families had to leave their houses because of the mud, so they moved into the school gym and slept on army cots. The volcano was all anybody could talk about.

Laura had one of the best stories to tell, not only because she was one of the last people on the mountain, but also because she had been one of the last who talked to Harry.

Some of the other kids had good stories too. Up near the mountain some had seen rocks the size of walnuts tumbling down from the sky. There was so much ash in the air that even when the street lights went on in town nobody could see anything. The ash was like snow, except it didn't melt. And it was heavy, especially when it got wet. Some people's roofs caved in. The police closed all the roads and nobody could drive for three days. Cranes worked around the clock, riverside.

Cindy Leighton had one of the strangest stories. She said the mud from the river flowed right in their front door and through their living room. Then it filled up the kitchen and went down the hall and into the bedrooms, right over the blankets and everything.

Laura didn't believe her at first, but one day after school she went out to the house with Cindy.

Sure enough. They had to duck their heads just to get in the front door. Inside, the mud had hardened, and it was just like cement. Outside, where Laura and Cindy used to play basketball, the mud went all the way up the backboard. You could walk right over and sit down on the hoop.

All summer long the derricks worked down by the river, big diggers and buckets on cables that workers used to dig out a trench for the river to go in. They were afraid if they didn't get it dug out, all the water would flow into town.

Laura and Willie watched the workers from their back yard. From there, they looked like a swarm of ants, scurrying around and making big piles of dirt.

Nobody could go up to the mountain or Spirit Lake, nobody except scientists and reporters and rescue people. The highway that went to Spirit Lake, the one the caravan had been on, was washed out or buried in mud. All the bridges over the river were gone. Helicopters were the only way to get up there.

Carlos had to go up all the time, to do research. He said there were scientists from all over the country studying what was happening. He had moved into a trailer house just outside of town so he could be closer to the volcano, and he started coming around the house often with lots of information about what was happening on the mountain.

When they saw him right after he had come down for the day he would be covered with ash. It would be everywhere, in his hair and shoes and even his ears. He said it was very hot and dusty up there and just about every living thing was gone. The trees had been blown down and their leaves burned up by the heat. All that was left was the big tree trunks, criss-crossed like hundreds of pick-up sticks.

Carlos was excited about it, though.

The mountain only *looked* dead, he said. When you studied it closely, he told them, you could see that all kinds of plants and animals were coming back to live there.

Although almost all the animals had been killed by the eruption, Carlos said, a few of them — frogs and lizards and fish that had been in lakes covered with ice, and some animals that lived underground — had survived.

One that Carlos was very excited about was the pocket gopher. Pocket gophers were furry little animals about the size of hamsters, and they were living underground in their tunnels when the mountain erupted. That protected them, even though everything above them was blown away or covered with ash. Carlos discovered that the pocket gophers were still doing fine. They were eating the roots of plants that still stuck down below the ground, and other food they had stored.

"Not only that," Carlos told them, "but they're helping other things live. When they dig, they mix ash with the rich soil buried under it, so they make these nice little garden spots where plants can grow."

"But where do the seeds come from?" Laura asked.

"From the air," he said. "They float in on the wind, some of them from miles away."

The seeds were landing on the dirt plowed by the gophers, and bursting into bloom. "There are all kinds of places like that up there," Carlos said, "they're like oases in a desert."

Whenever Laura or Willie asked about Harry, Carlos said there really wasn't much of a chance that he was alive. When the volcano erupted, the whole side of the mountain next to Spirit Lake just slid down, right into the lake. All the cabins and the lodge and everything were totally covered up. The lake was still there, but it was full of dead logs and there was nothing around it but ash.

Laura thought about Harry quite a bit. She secretly believed he had made it up to his hidey hole in the cliff and that someday soon, when nobody was expecting it, he would come walking out. Once she even dreamed that Harry came walking down the mountain, carrying a walking stick and leading all of his cats in a long line. He had cleaned out the lodge, he told her, and he hoped she would come and visit when they all came up to the cabin that summer. "And bring Catman," he said. "I want to see if you're taking good care of him."

When she told Carlos the dream, he looked concerned. "You know that was just a dream, right?"

"Of course," she said. How could she not know, she was the one who had dreamed it.

"But I mean, you realize that Harry could never open the lodge again, and that you will never see the cabin again?"

Laura didn't say anything. You never knew anything for sure, it seemed.

After that, Carlos started talking to Mama about how it might be a good idea to see if he could get permission to take Laura and Willie up to the mountain, so they could see for themselves what had happened.

The idea of actually going up to look at the volcano, close up, sounded wonderful to Laura and Willie. But Mama didn't think it was safe. "If it's safe, how come they make you carry radios?" she asked Carlos. "And if they can tell when it's going to erupt again, why couldn't they tell last time?"

She didn't really believe that Carlos would actually be able to get permission anyway. "You said yourself they're hardly letting anybody go up. Why would they let two kids go?"

Charlie said that his boss, the man who organized all the scientists, had been a good friend of Harry's, and that might make some difference.

"We'll see," was all Mama would say.

Chapter Eight
The Living Mountain

To everybody's amazement, Carlos's boss said it was okay if they went up to the mountain — not just Laura and Willie, but Mama, too.

"I think it was talking about Harry that did it," Carlos said. "He told me, 'Well, any kid that Harry bothered talking to must be some kid.' "

That made Laura feel good. "What about Catman?" she asked. "Can he come too?"

"I think Catman better sit this one out," Carlos said. "Cats don't like helicopters."

Laura and Willie had never been in a helicopter before, and they could hardly wait. Especially Willie. All the way to the field outside of town, where the pilot said he would pick them up, Willie bounced in his seat like a happy rabbit.

The pilot's name was Jesse, and when they climbed inside the helicopter, he helped strap them all in. Laura got to sit up front with Jesse, and Mama, Carlos and Willie squeezed into the back.

Jesse handed them each some headphones with a microphone and a cord with a button on it. "It'll be too noisy when we get going to talk without these," he said.

Jesse closed the doors, flicked a few switches and said something into the radio. Then suddenly they were in the air. It was like magic.

Laura had been in airplanes before, but being in a helicopter was like riding inside a glass bubble. You could see everywhere. They sailed over the trees and houses and everything shrank below them.

"We'll just follow the river right up to the mountain," Jesse's voice came into the headphones. He pointed below them. "This is where the old highway was, right in there."

Laura looked down and saw broken sections of the road they had taken on the day the caravan of cars went up the mountain — the day they had met Carlos and she had followed Catman to Harry's place. All that seemed like years ago now, almost as if it had happened to somebody else.

What had been the river was now a wide stripe of gray where the mud had poured down from the mountain. The big shovels and trucks working to dig out the river channel looked like toys in a sandbox.

They followed the flow of mud as it wound through green forests and climbed toward the volcano. Then, suddenly, the green disappeared. The world turned into black and white, like an old movie on television. The forest was still standing, but all the trees were dead. Their branches were shriveled into curlicues from the heat.

Closer to the mountain the trees were lying down flat, their trunks criss-crossed on top of each other and partly covered with ash. Then there were no trees at all, only gray earth, with the river, also gray, snaking through deep canyons cut into the ash.

Laura tried to remember what it had been like before. She thought about the cool, green forests and remembered the mother deer and two fawns she had seen on the way up to the cabin that last time.

She glanced back at Carlos again. She couldn't believe he thought it was so wonderful up here. Everything was dead.

Mama must have been thinking the same thing. "It's so sad."

"Just wait," Carlos answered.

Jesse turned the helicopter slightly and there beside them was

Mount St. Helens, or what was left of it. The whole top was gone and the mountain was hollowed out inside like an old caved-in hat. Wisps of steam were rising from inside the crater.

Laura looked for Spirit Lake. She couldn't see it at first because she was looking for something green, like the water used to be. She saw the lake at last, and it was gray, like everything else.

Jesse pointed into the crater. "New dome," he said.

Laura looked inside the crater and there, right in the middle, was a little miniature mountain.

"There's the new Mount St. Helens," Carlos explained. "That's where the melted rock comes out from underground and hardens. Every time there's an eruption it grows a little bigger. Someday it'll fill up the whole crater, and there will be a whole new mountain.

"Can't get too close," Jesse said. "Bad updrafts." He swung the helicopter around and set it down on a big white plain between the lake and the mountain.

A cloud of fine white ash rose around them. "Right down in there is where the cabins were," he said, pointing toward the lake.

Jesse shut off the engine and Laura took off her headphones. Suddenly it was very quiet. When the dust had settled they climbed out of the helicopter and stood on the ground. Laura felt shaky and mixed up, as if they were explorers who had just landed on another planet.

Willie hit the ground running, like a little dog off its leash. "I can't believe it; look at this," he kept saying, over and over.

"I'll wait here," Jesse said. He walked around the helicopter, checking struts and cables. "You guys go on ahead."

Carlos picked up the pack with their lunch in it and led them slowly away from the helicopter, across crunchy little stones the size of marbles. Willie stopped and picked up a handful of them. "Hey, these rocks don't weigh anything," he said. "They feel like popcorn or something." He started filling his pockets.

"Pumice," Carlos said. "It's rock that cooled so fast it got mixed up with air. Come on. I'll take you down to where your cabin was." They crunched their way across the pumice, heading toward the lake. As they walked, Laura saw that what had looked so bare and dead from the air was not actually dead at all. Little green plants poked out of the ash all around them. In some places, big bunches of yellow flowers made splotches of bright color against the ash. They were the same as flowers Laura had seen in their backyard at home. They didn't seem at all special there. But up here, surrounded by grey, they looked like miracles. When she stopped to smell one bunch of flowers, she saw a bee bouncing from blossom to blossom.

"How did this bee get way up here?" she asked Carlos.

"It flew or drifted in on the wind," he said. "Insects were some of the first living things to come back after the eruption. Jesse was in here two days after it blew up.

He said there were already wasps and flies buzzing around. Sometimes when the wind is blowing you can see spiders drifting on pieces of their webs, just like hang gliders."

"How do they live?" Laura asked. "What do they eat ?"

"Most of them don't live very long. But they make good food for other animals — like birds. And when they die, their bodies help fertilize the ground, so more plants can grow. It all works together."

They walked sideways down a steep ravine, their feet sliding in the powdery ash. At the bottom was a stream that ran down from the mountain. The rocks along the banks were covered with bright orange growth that looked like fur. Laura had never seen anything like it.

Willie was down on his hands and knees, staring at the orange growth and poking it with his finger. "What's this stuff, Carlos?"

"Algae. Put your hand in the water."

Willie did and quickly pulled it out again, surprised. "It's hot!"

"The rocks underground are still heated up there," Carlos said, pointing to the crater. "They heat up the streams and make some really weird things grow. On the other side of the lake there's a place where steam comes out and keeps everything warm and moist all the time. We call it 'Fumerole Gardens' because there's ferns and all sorts of things growing there. Come on, though, I want to show you my favorite project."

He led them across the stream, dancing from rock to rock without getting his feet wet. He scrambled up the bank on the other side and then stood there on top, waiting for them.

When Laura got to the top and looked over the other side, she gasped. There was a bright purple field of flowers, stretching nearly to the lake shore. The air was filled with the sound of bees at work, and birds flitted back and forth.

"Oh, Carlos, it's beautiful," Mama said. "It really is just like an oasis. How did it get here?"

"Remember when I told you about the pocket gophers?" Carlos asked proudly. "Well, they plowed up a nice little garden right here after the mountain blew up last May. One single little lupine plant got started and then all these other ones took over. I've been watching it spread ever since I first started coming up here."

"All this started with one plant?" Willie said, staring.

"That's right. It spread out and when it got big enough it started catching other seeds that blew by. They started growing next to it. It caught insects, too, and birds flew in to eat the insects. Coyotes and elk and all kinds of other animals saw it from a long ways away and they came over to explore."

"Just one summer, and already there's this whole garden up here. There are little places like this all over. Gradually, they're all spreading toward each other. Pretty soon they'll join and there will be plants everywhere. The trees will get bigger and in a hundred years or so the whole place will look like a forest again."

"A hundred years?" Willie said. He looked disappointed. "We'll all be dead by then."

"Well, yes, that's true. But our grandkids, and great-grandkids, will be around. They'll look at the woods and say, 'Wow, just think, this used to all be completely bare right after the volcano blew up. I wish I could have seen it then.' "

Laura had not thought of it that way. It seemed to make sense, but she still felt terrible about Harry.

"Where would Harry's place have been?" she asked.

Carlos was bringing out the lunch — sandwiches, apples and juice. He sat up and looked around. "It's hard to say, exactly, everything is so different. As near as I can tell though, I think your cabin would have been right in there somewhere." He pointed to a tangle of broken tree trunks near the lake. "Harry's place would be back by that stream, except about three hundred feet underground."

After lunch, Carlos and Willie went down to the lake shore to hunt for salamanders. Willie had told Carlos he had decided to be a scientist when he grew up.

Laura didn't know what she wanted to be. She lay on her back, staring up at the volcano and the blue sky. Clouds of steam drifted lazily out of the crater. When they got to the rim, the wind caught them and spread them into lacy patterns. How short a cloud's life is, she thought. It's born, blows around a little and then it's gone.

Mama was sitting still, too, gazing across the lake.

"I'm going over to where Harry's place was," Laura told her.

Mama nodded. "Be careful," she said. "And come right back."

Laura walked back to the stream by herself. When she got to the spot where Carlos said Harry's lodge was, she stopped and stood there, looking up at what was left of the mountain and thinking about Harry, feeding his cats on his front steps. She felt her throat get tight. A tear ran down her cheek.

She sat down on the ground to think. Next to her, in the shelter of a rock, was a tiny fir tree, no bigger than her hand, its little green needles soft and tender. Harry seemed so real right then that she could almost see him, when he had pointed at the mountain and told her, "The end of one thing is only the beginning of something else."

"You were right, Harry." she said out loud.

Laura lay down on her stomach and put her head on her arms so she could see the little tree better. On one tiny branch she saw a spot of bright orange with black dots. A ladybug. She touched the tips of her fingers to her lips and blew it a kiss.

"Good luck, little lady," she whispered.

EPILOGUE

Mt. St. Helens erupted in 1980 with the force of 27,000 atom bombs. In a matter of hours, the blast flattened or vaporized 234 square miles of forest. Almost all life on the mountain disappeared.

Harry Truman, a real person, died in the eruption and was buried under a ridge that now bears his name.

In the short time since the eruption, nature has made a remarkable recovery. Already much of the land is covered with new plants. Islands of fireweed and lupine now grace the ash-laden slopes, and creatures from pocket gophers to elk make their homes in the shadow of the volcano. The water in Spirit Lake is once again clear and clean.

Scientists from around the world travel to Mt. St. Helens to study how plants and animals have worked together to transform the mountain.

ABOUT THE AUTHOR

Rob Carson worked as a surveyor for the U.S. Forest Service in the old-growth forests that surrounded Mt. St. Helens before the volcano erupted. Later, as a journalist in Seattle, he wrote many stories about the eruption and the recovery of the mountain. In 1990, he wrote the widely acclaimed book, Mt. St. Helens, the Eruption and Recovery of a Volcano. He was nominated for a Pulitzer Prize for his writing in 1992.

Carson lives on Bainbridge Island with his wife, Lyn, his daughter, Theodora, and their cat, George.